Sea Habitats

Julie Haydon

Chapter 1	What Is a Habitat?	2
Chapter 2	Habitat: Rock Pool	4
Chapter 3	Habitat: Coral Reef	8
Chapter 4	Habitat: Open Sea	12
Chapter 5	Habitat: Deep-sea Floor	16
Chapter 6	Habitat: Polar Seas	20
Glossary and Index		24

Chapter 1
What Is a Habitat?

A habitat is the place where an animal lives, eats and has its babies. Some animals stay in the one habitat all the time. Other animals move in and out of their habitats.

habitat: rock pool

habitat: coral reef

Most of Earth is covered in salt water. The salt water makes up the seas. There are different habitats in the seas. Many animals live in these habitats.

habitat: open sea

habitat: polar sea

Chapter 2
Habitat: Rock Pool

Some beaches are covered in rocks. Sometimes there are pools of water in the rocks. These pools are called rock pools.

When the **tide** comes in, water goes into a rock pool. When the tide goes out, water is left behind in the rock pool.

Some rock pools have water in them all the time. Other rock pools dry up. They fill with water again when the tide comes in.

Some animals live in rock pools all the time. Other animals move in and out of different rock pools.

octopus

sponge

fish

sea snail

A closer look:

Some plankton live in rock pools. Plankton are tiny plants and animals that **float** together in the sea. Some sea animals eat plankton.

Chapter 3
Habitat: Coral Reef

Coral reefs are found in warm seas. Coral animals are called **polyps**. A coral reef is made up of polyps and the **skeletons** of dead polyps.

Some polyps have their skeletons on the outside of their bodies. When these polyps die, their skeletons are left behind. New polyps build on the skeletons. This makes the reef grow.

A coral reef is a good place to live. There are lots of plants and animals to eat. There are many places to hide too.

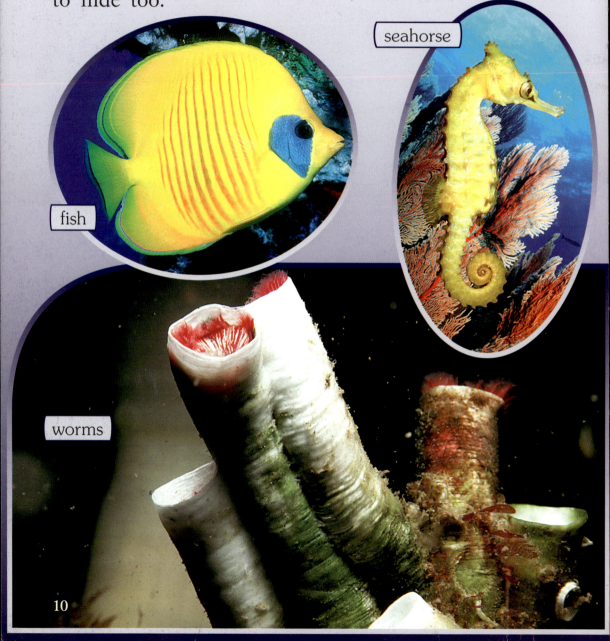

A closer look:

Some sea stars, or starfish, live in coral reefs. A sea star has many arms. If a sea star's arm is pulled off, it can grow a new one.

Chapter 4

Habitat: Open Sea

The open sea is far from land. It can be very deep. Sometimes animals that live in the open sea swim a long way to find food.

It is hard to hide in the open sea. Some fish live in large groups in the open sea. This helps the fish stay safe because they can all watch for enemies.

Some animals that live in the open sea move closer to land to have their babies.

A closer look:

Some fish live in the open sea. Most fish have **scales** on their bodies. They have fins to help them swim. They have gills so they can breathe in water.

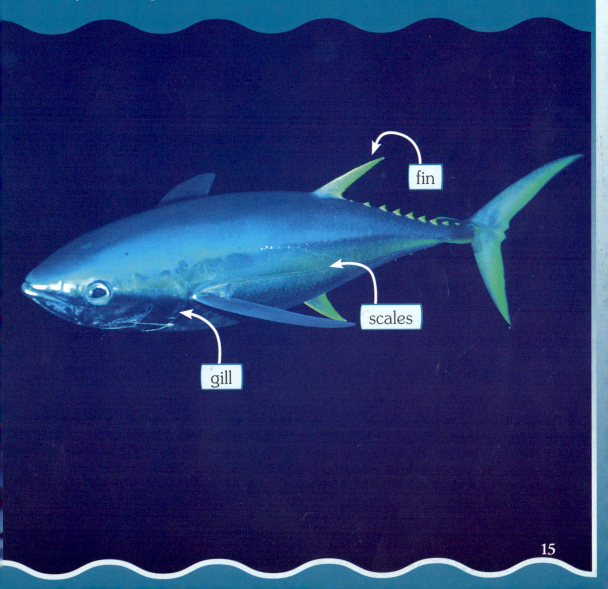

Chapter 5
Habitat: Deep-sea Floor

The deep-sea floor is the deepest part of the sea. It is so deep that it does not get any sunlight. No plants can grow on the deep-sea floor.

deep-sea vent

Most of the deep sea is cold. In some places, hot water comes out of **vents** on the sea floor. Some animals live near the vents. These animals cannot live in other habitats.

Many of the animals that live near the vents are white.

A closer look:

Giant tube worms live near vents on the deep-sea floor. Each worm makes a tube to live in. Giant tube worms can grow taller than a man!

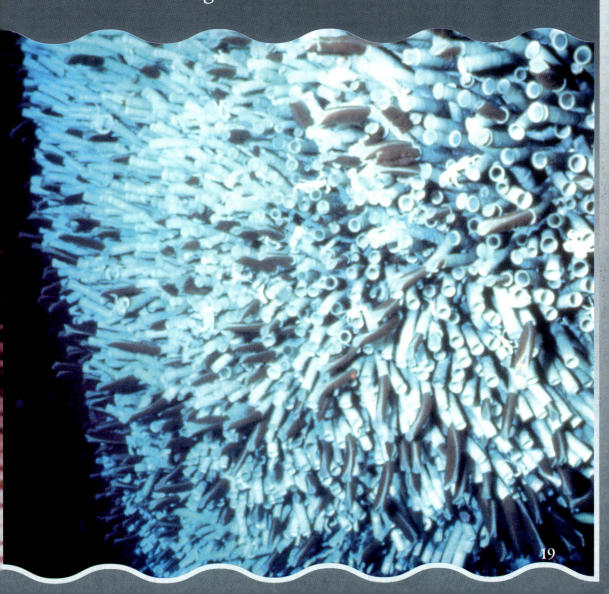

Chapter 6
Habitat: Polar Seas

There are two **poles** on Earth. There is the North Pole and the South Pole. It is cold and icy at the poles.

Some animals live in the seas near the poles. Some of these animals spend some time on land. Animals in the polar seas can live in very cold water.

Here are some of the sea animals that live near the South Pole.

A closer look:

Some whales spend time in polar seas. A whale is not a fish, it is a **mammal**. It must breathe air. A whale has one or two **blowholes** on the top of its head. It lifts its head out of the water to breathe through the blowholes.

Glossary

blowholes	holes at the top of a whale's head that help it breathe
float	to lie or move on the top of water without sinking
mammal	animals that give birth to live babies and make milk for their babies
poles	areas of land at the most northern and southern points on Earth
polyps	coral animals whose skeletons make up coral reefs
scales	flat, thin plates that cover fish and some other animals
skeletons	hard frameworks made of bones or other materials that are part of the bodies of some animals
tide	the rise and fall of the sea
vents	holes that let out air, smoke, gas or water

Index

fish 6, 10, 13, 15, 18
giant tube worms 18, 19
plankton 7
poles 20–21, 22
polyps 8–9

sea star 11
salt water 3
tide 4, 5
vents 17–18, 19
whale 23